JAN BRETT
Trouble with Trolls

G. P. Putnam's Sons

New York

For my sister, Sophie

with thanks to Abbie Sullivan

Printed in Hong Kong by South China Printing Co. (1988) Ltd.
Type design by Patrick Collins. The text is set in Garamond #3.
Airbrush backgrounds by Joseph Hearne.
Library of Congress Cataloging-in-Publication Data
Brett, Jan,   The trouble with trolls / Jan Brett.   p.   cm.   Summary: While
climbing Mt. Baldy, Treva outwits some trolls who want to steal her dog.   [1.
Trolls—Fiction.] I. Title PZ7.B7559Tr 1992 [E]—dc20 91-41061 CIP AC
ISBN: 0-399-22336-3

5   7   9   10   8   6

My name is Treva, and I have had trouble with trolls.

It all happened one day in early spring when I decided to visit my cousin who lives on the other side of Mount Baldy. It takes all morning to climb up the mountain, but then I fly down the other side on my skis.

My dog, Tuffi, and I walked up the path until we reached the place where the last of the old trees stood. And that's where the trouble with trolls began.

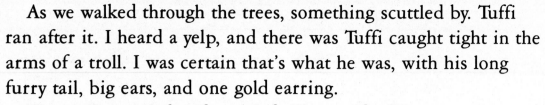

As we walked through the trees, something scuttled by. Tuffi ran after it. I heard a yelp, and there was Tuffi caught tight in the arms of a troll. I was certain that's what he was, with his long furry tail, big ears, and one gold earring.

The troll squealed and growled. "I want dog!"

He waggled his ears back and forth at me. Then I had an idea.
Maybe I could trick this greedy troll. "Go ahead. Take the dog.
I've got my beautiful mittens." And I reached up and warmed my
ears as if I couldn't do without my mittens.

The troll's eyes darted back and forth from Tuffi to my mittens.
But it was too much. He had to have them. He dropped Tuffi,
grabbed my mittens, and ran off.

I was so pleased about tricking the troll that I didn't notice that Tuffi was missing again until I came face to face with a second troll. This one was rocking with glee, his long nose buried in Tuffi's warm fur.

"I got dog!" he boasted.

I shrugged. "Oh, you can have the dog," I said. "Just don't take my favorite pom-pom hat." I fluffed it up and dusted my nose with it.

The troll's eyes lit up. He snatched the hat and scurried away as fast as he could go.

What a morning. I had lived on Mount Baldy all of my life, and I had never heard of anyone ever seeing a troll. It was time to take steps.

"Tuffi," I ordered. "From now on, you follow me."

What I didn't know was that a third troll was sneaking up behind us. I heard a noise.

Woop! This troll had grabbed Tuffi by the tail and was pointing to a big iron pot.

"Pull, pull!" she cried.

I slipped off my sweater when she wasn't looking.

"Whew!" I said. "That leaves my special puller." I put a rock down the neck of my sweater and pulled it by the arms to show how it worked.

Trolls are dim, but this one was smart enough to see that my sweater was just the thing to drag her pot. She scampered away with it, and Tuffi and I listened to the *bong, bong, bong* of the pot bouncing down the mountain.

Now we could see the top of Mount Baldy. What a relief! What we didn't know was that we were walking toward double trouble.

As Tuffi and I squeezed between two boulders, twin trolls jumped out.

"Ha! Ha!" they bellowed together, and pounced on Tuffi.

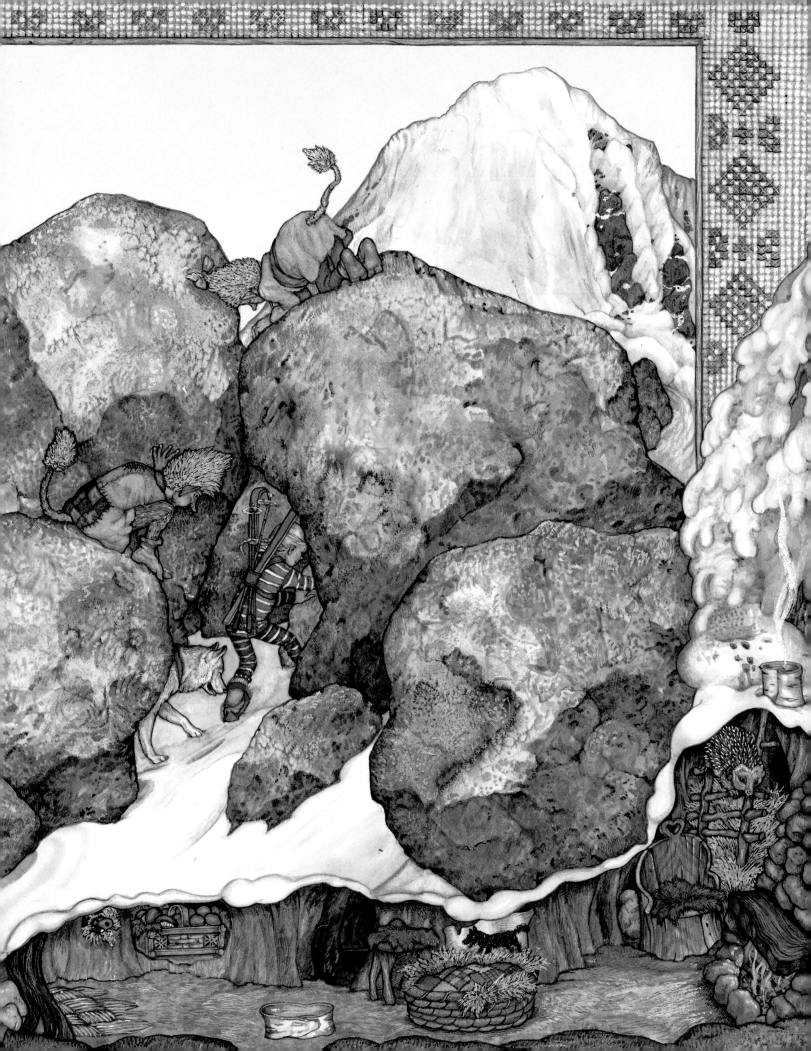

This time I was ready. I saw their pointy little heads and knew just what to do. Off came my boots. I dangled them in the air.

"Imagine wanting a dog and ignoring these."

Instantly the twin trolls dropped Tuffi and leaped for my boots.

As they disappeared into the distance, I looked down at Tuffi. The top of the mountain was close. "I'm not taking any chances. I'm going to carry you the rest of the way."

Each step was harder. I held Tuffi tightly and kept going. When we reached the top, all five trolls were waiting.

"We want dog!" they bellowed, and ran toward us.

In the scuffle they got Tuffi away from me. I closed my eyes to keep back the tears.

Then I knew what to do. I reached around and unbuckled my skis. I held them so the sun would sparkle on their shiny paint. I shook them so the trolls could hear their tiny bells. I waved them through the air, making a *swoosh, swoosh* sound. Finally I whispered, as if it were a big secret, "I can fly with these."

"Fly!" the trolls roared. "How fly?"

I picked up my ski poles. I blew on my hands to warm them. "I'll need my mittens to show you."

The troll with the big ears threw my mittens over.

"I can't fly unless I can see," I said reluctantly. "I'll need my hat to keep the wind from blowing my hair in my eyes."

The troll with the long nose tossed me my pom-pom hat.

"Look," I said, shivering in the wind. "Flying is easy, but I can't do it without my sweater. And that's final."

The other trolls stared at the troll with my sweater. She hesitated but then gave it to me. I put it on and positioned my skis on the snow. But even the trolls could see that my feet wouldn't fit into the bindings.

"I really need those boots," I said reassuringly to the twins.

Now I had everything back—my mittens, my hat, my sweater, my boots. I stood at the top of Mount Baldy ready to go. I held a piece of yarn high in the air to test the wind for flying. It was too much for those greedy trolls.

"Fly! Fly! Fly!" they clamored.

"I need you to push me."

"Can't push!" they cried. "Hold dog!"

"Okay," I said, sighing. "I'll hold the dog."

The trolls gave me one giant push.

"Fly! Fly! Fly!" they shouted at me.

As we flew down the mountain, I could hear the trolls' cries change to wails of "Dog! Dog! Dog!"

And as I looked back, all I could see was a pile of trolls shoving and pushing each other furiously around in the snow, arms flying, heads bumping.

Tuffi and I made it safely down the mountain, and the trolls have never been seen again. But if you travel over the top of Mount Baldy in early spring, you can see the white cotton grass waving wildly in the wind. It's all that is left from the day I had the trouble with trolls.